Dr. Chuckle's

ORIGINAL
CINEMA
555 PUNS

Dr. Chuckle's

ORIGINAL CINEMA

555 PUNS

Paul Frishkoff

Dr. Chuckle's Original Cinema: 555 Puns
© 2020 Paul Frishkoff

ISBN: 978-1-943190-21-8

Wild Ginger Press
www.wildgingerpress.com

Dedication

MY FANS – big thanks to you both – may recall that I dedicated each of my first two books to recently deceased acquaintances. So, I said to my equally weird brother Bruce, "If you pre-decease me, I'll dedicate the next book to you, but if I pre-decease, I'll dedicate it to me." As neither eventuality occurred before we went to press, this book is dedicated to the late Coconut, pet frog to my son Luke and his wife Alison. They rescued Coconut from a drying puddle in 2011 along with five of his siblings. Alas (appetite-spoiler alert!), the voracious frog consumed them all! (As a noted batrachologist* observed: "One frog's croak is another frog's croquette".) He also ate lettuce (courtesy of his "romaine man") and insects (though not always cricket). Coconut was a chorus frog *(Pseudacris regilla)*. He had no known opportunity to court little chorus-girl frogs, but no doubt would have opened with: "Wanna come up and see my pad?" His favorite bedtime story was "The Tail of Peter Ribbit". Though usually confined to a terrarium, he was rarely des-pond-ent and lived a long and hoppy life, expiring of old age. His mummified remains were illicitly buried in a spot in nature which Dr. Chuckle is sworn not to divulge. Now, as we kiss him farewell, he is magically turned into print.

---

*frog expert

Preface

FILMS HAVE BEEN an integral part of my life. My first childhood trip to a theater was to see "Lassie Come Home", during which – I've been told – I yelled out "Let that dog go, you mean men!"

I've watched the Oscars sporadically; not so much lately. My wife Pat, however, is an ardent watcher and this book is inspired by her. Moreover, she has been the main auditory guinea pig for the puns in this and my prior two books.

The format is a selected list of Best Film nominees over the years with two puns accompanying each, chosen to match the film's title and – occasionally – its content.

About originality: I have very good recall; as far as I know, each pun in this book (and my other two pun books) is "original" in the sense that I haven't heard or read any of them before. (The two exceptions are prominently asterisked.) However, given a couple of billion English speakers in the world, it is debatable that no one, nowhere, could have had the same thought as I did.

About delectability: puns, in my experience, are most easily digested if read sparsely, no more than two a day. Gluttons beware! If you don't "get" a pun, try saying it out loud. (You can practice on some of the attributions at the end of this preface.)

This book was produced and directed by Bobbi Benson, with the epic flair of a Cecil B. DeMille (or, at least, a William Castle). Janet Gelernter served as "gaffer", carefully proofreading and shedding light on numerous errata. The support staff was led by Al Famayl, humbly aided by Rankin File. Our copyright advisor was Hans Orff. Cowboy stunt work was by Russell Steers. The staff peppy yoga trainer is Amber Dextrose. Dental advice is by Ginger Vitus. Our recordkeeper is Vic Troller. Jazz history was compiled by Bertha DeBlooze. Obits were drafted by N. Lou of Flowers. Our snoopy next-door neighbor is Eudora Wazoo-Penn. The occasional miracle is courtesy of Ray Zdeded. Our nostalgic "party girl" is Dacia Wynan-Rosas. Hotel security from Enoch Zondors. Athletic support provided by Jacques Trapp. Natalie R. Aide served as fashion consultant.

Note to the Reader

These icons will indicated winners or nominees.

Best picture winner

Best picture nominee

Foreign film winner

Foreign film nominee

Wings
1927-8

Who was Audubon?
A Wren-aissance man.

Which bird has the most nervous stomach?
The up-chukar.

The Love Parade
1929-30

What did the call girl say to reassure the gambler?
"Head you win, tail you win."

How did he try to have a hot time with the hibachi chef?
He put his hand under her brazier.

The Front Page
1930-31

Where can you read about the World
Weightlifting Championships?
In the Bench Press.

What did the arch-rival chefs do in their food columns?
They panned each other.

Bad Girl
1931-32

What are the sounds emanating from brothels?
The din of iniquity.

Why was the call girl's shift from 10 a.m. to 3 p.m.?
She worked bonkers' hours.

The Champ
1931-32

What's a common poker bluff by cannibals?
"I'll sear you and braise you!"

On what TV show did competitors defame each other?
"What's Malign?"

One Hour with You
1931-32

Who is the most fickle of lovers?
"One-Night" Stan.

Why did he eat every meal at Papa John's?
He wanted a pizza ass.

Little Women
1932-33, 2020

Why was Humbert Humbert obsessed with Lolita?
She was urchin him on.

Why did the waifs like to listen to Carmina Burana?
They were Orff-fans.

Smilin' Through
1932-33

What does a commuter do when the
outbound train is very delayed?
Sip suburban or two.

What did the dentist say to forewarn
the highway engineer?
"Bridge work ahead!"

She Done Him Wrong
1932-33

When did they mistake adhesive for KY?
On a dark and glue-me night.

Why is the horny teen cheerleader still remembered?
She went down in History.

It Happened One Night
1934

What did the charitable strumpet have?
A community chest.

What happened after they located Dracula's castle?
Interest in him quickly spiked; the stakes were high.

Cleopatra
1934, 1963

What did the mummy couple like to do?
Gauze into each other's eyes.

Where did Cleopatra hang out in San Francisco?
On top of the Mark.

Imitation of Life
1934

"I just saw a new movie about eunuchs."
"And how did the cast rate?"

How did the necrophiliac chess master cope?
He had a stale mate.

One Night of Love
1934

Where do you order a golden shower?
From UPS.

What gift did the King of Norway offer to Ophelia?
Four tin bras.

Captain Blood
1935

How do you feel after being punched by a sailor?
Gobsmacked.

What do you get when you cross Popeye
with the Energizer Bunny?
A salt and battery.

Top Hat
1935

"Do you recall ever being scalped?"
"Not off the top of my head."

Why did he collect women's berets?
He was a latent hat-ero-sexual.

The Informer
1935

Why did the celeb suddenly lose acclaim?
Her extolled on her.
(She lost De Laud.)

What did Jabba the Hutt do when his
girlfriend ratted on him?
"Smoked" his hooker.

Libeled Lady
1936

Which French heroine egged on her lovers?
Mme Ovary.

What did the English speaker wear to the Paris Opera?
A 'lame' dress.
(Her obtuse date wore a boot in ear.)

The Awful Truth
1937

How did the paver develop hemorrhoids?
They were due to an asphalt.

What are peons called in Detroit?
Pistons.

The Good Earth
1937

What did the miner tell his staff when his neighbor
wanted to borrow equipment?
"Hidey hoe!"

What made her think that the shrub was a mimosa?
It was acacia mistaken identity.

A Star Is Born
1937

What did the environmentalist do in the string band?
Played the ecolele.

What is the most uncouth Broadway musical?
"A Coarse Line."

Stage Door
1937

What did he say when he caught his girlfriend in bed
with the mezzo-soprano?
"What's a girl like you doing in a diva like that?"

Who was the portliest rock star?
Fats Abdominal.

Grand Illusion
1938

"I come from such a small town that:

- *the city limits signs are back-to-back;*
- *the village green is a divot;*
- *the town crier only whimpers;*
- *the municipal sewer system has a half-moon on the door;*
- *the mayoral race is between a schizophrenic;*
- *the village idiot is shared with three other towns;*
- *the local cow is a Half-stein;*
- *everyone's family tree is identical;*
- *uptown is located downtown.*"

(Author's note: The late Rodney Dangerfield, whose show I saw in Toronto years back, delivered these additional gems: "The pawnbroker's sign has only one ball; the town hooker is a virgin.")

The Adventures of Robin Hood
1938

Why did Little John cross paths with Robin Hood?
He was too big for his bridges.

First duelist: "Crime does not epee!"
Second duelist: "It does, too, Shea!"

Gone with the Wind
1939

What did exhibitionists do in the Confederacy?
Whistled Dick-see.

Why did Scarlett make nasty jokes
about her acquaintances?
It was just her ha-style.

Dark Victory
1939

Why is it dangerous to use an oil filter for birth control?
Someone could die-of-Fram.

How do you learn more about the
author of "Dead Souls"?
You simply Google "Gogol".

Of Mice and Men
1939

What were Sir Thomas Lipton's last words?
"God, all my tea!"

What do vegan men wear to formal weddings?
Cucumberbunds.

The Letter
1940

What kind of blood do bad keyboarders have?
Typo.

"Who keeps mailing me lewd spam?"
"It might be some whore, Mel."

Our Town
1940

What are the MapQuest directions to Ye Olde Tea Shoppe?
"Just park oolong the curb and take a pekoe through the window.
Beware! The Earl Grey merde ain't what it used to be!"

What does "Liar, liar, pants on fire" mean?
"You're burning your britches behind you!"

One Foot in Heaven
1941

Where did the indigent priest buy his vestments?
At the shrift store.

What did the band play during the Last Supper?
"Sting low, Iscariot."

Suspicion
1941

Why was she dissatisfied with the
hunky sleuth whom she hired?
He was a private defective.

Why did they stop surveillance of the spinning larvae?
There's no sense spying over milled silk.

The Talk of the Town
1942

How do perverts do research?
They use Wicked Pedia.

What did the trash-talking basketball player do?
She driveled before she shot.

Yankee Doodle Dandy
1942

Who sang bass and soprano, and built a canal?
Duet Clinton.

Why did the strait-laced politician sing rap music at rallies?
It was hip-hop-crisy.

The Human Comedy
1943

What was the highlight of the gastroenterologist
convention at Vegas?
The crapshoot.

What did the bullock think when the brainy halfwit
walked into the pasture?
"Ox See Moron."

In Which We Serve
1943

What do breakfast cooks wear in the Rockies?
Denver armlets.

What do picketers do when their knees give out?
They're walking on aches.

The More the Merrier
1943

Why did the hoarder keep no tacky art
or mineral supplements?
She had everything but the kitsch and zinc.

What did the courtesan like on her pasta?
Pecker-ino sauce.

Going My Way
1944

"Tacoma is the second largest city in Washington."
"I think you misspoke, Anne."

What did one Croat tell the other?
"Let Zagreb something to eat."

Gaslight
1944

Why do cabbage and cauliflower produce noisy toots?
They're vociferous vegetables.

Why do some woodwind players fart into the mouthpieces?
They don't know their ass from their oboe.

Double Indemnity
1944

To what did the San Francisco pastry chef succumb?
The Great Bay-Cough.

What happened when he sat on a frozen waffle?
He got a little Eggo-testicle.

Since You Went Away
1944

What was the outcome of the marital triangle?
Polly gone.

What do ditzy people do for vacations?
They stay at Airhead-bnb's.

Anchors Aweigh
1945

What did Captain Hook say to the crocodile?
He made offhand comments.

What did the shabby oarsman do?
Rowed a dingy.

Great Expectations
1947

Who is the biggest optimist at Hialeah?
Parlay Anna.

"Hello, Russell, I'm the carpenter you sent for."
"The time has come to wall," Russ said.

Shoe Shine
1947

What did the dermatologist wear to the gym?
Her black Keds.

Where did Hiawatha buy his loafers?
From the stores of Gucci-gimme.

The Snake Pit
1948

Who remands possessed people to the "funny farm?"
Judge Mental.

How did he react to the diagnosis of dual-personality?
He was beside himself.

All the King's Men
1949

"That was a foul political campaign you ran, Sid."
"But I rank #1 with the voters and will be fetid by them!"

Why did critics knock the Humpty Dumpty movie?
They said that the plot was off the wall.

Twelve O'Clock High
1949

What's another way of saying "12:54"?
"Half a dozen of the other."

What Duke Ellington tune is used for insomnia ads?
"In a Melatonin."

All About Eve
1950

Where was the first cheese produced?
The Garden of Edam.

Why was Cain such a rascal?
He was imp-elled.

Born Yesterday
1950

"Our new flooring salesperson seems rather ignorant."
"How little does Lynn know, Liam?"

What do infants get from eating dog meat?
Collie.

Decision before Dawn
1951

How long did it take the invaders to overrun the citadel?
About a fort-night.

What beer did the sports bar drinkers
order just before closing?
Their last round draft choice.

A Place in the Sun
1951

Who cornered the short-term rental market in Mecca?
The Sheikh of Air-bnb.

Who saved the day in Upper Michigan?
A deus ex mackinaw.

The Greatest Show on Earth
1952

What was Paul Bunyan's favorite timber festival event?
The climb-ax.

First actor on opening night: "Break a leg!"
Second actor: "Krakatoa!"

High Noon
1952

Who is the most notorious lamb rustler?
The Shepherd's Crook.

Who was hanged in Dodge City for bestiality?
An old cowpoke.

Forbidden Games
1952

What is the problem with anal sex?
It's hard to tell whether you're coming or going.

Where did ancient Greek harlots congregate?
In Spartan districts.

The Quiet Man
1952

What happened to the sailor who fell from the mast?
Rigger mortis.

What was the slogan of the laid-back toreador?
"Affable is better than none."

Julius Caesar
1953

"At what gate does Caesar's flight arrive, Cassius?"
"A-2, Brute!"

How did the Romans say: "Watch where you step"?
"Carpe B.M."

The Robe
1953

What happens to seamstresses who sit all day?
They have hem-a-rhoids.

What did the burly drycleaner have with his fiancée?
A pressing engagement.

On the Waterfront
1954

Where do ascetics go swimming?
The Celebes Sea.

Why did the dockworker punch the pushy
door-to-door salesman?
It was a vend-etta.

The Country Girl
1954

Who was the sweatiest frontierswoman?
Clammy-T Jane.

What did the Macedonian doctor warn her patient?
"I'm going to Skopje!"

Gate of Hell
1954

How did the islanders feel when their
coral reef was swept away?
It took atoll on them.

What was the dyslexic's favorite Civil War-era book?
"Knuckle Tom's Bacon."

Picnic
1955

Where did Colonel Sanders discover his secret ingredient?
In K-Y (while smoking blue grass).

Who gorged at the company picnic?
Aida Tall.

Around the World in 80 Days
1956

Why isn't wine packaged in Manila envelopes?
That's no way to fill-a-Pinot.

What's the most precarious location in Central Asia?
Between Iraq Kandahar place.

Friendly Persuasion
1956

How long did it take to purchase Manhattan?
About a New York Minuit.

Who markets cleansers for poopy diapers?
De turd gent.

Giant
1956

What befell the gluttonous giant?
He became meaty-ogre.

Why did people say that she was a real monster?
It had been bruted about.

12 Angry Men
1957

Why did the judge cancel his daily game of croquet?
*He had an absence of mallet and was libel to
contract hooping cough.*

What is a sadist's favorite dessert topping?
Cruel Whip.

Sayonara
1957

Why did Carrie Nation bring a hatchet to the saloons?
She liked razing the bar.

What befell the bawdy comic who insulted
the gang leader?
He was ribald with bullet holes.

Cat on a Hot Tin Roof
1958

Why beware of vengeful arsonists?
Their spark is worse than their spite.

How did she react to her first hot yoga session?
She said, "It's like asana in here!"

The Defiant Ones
1958

Who's in charge of security at Sing Sing?
Barb Dwyer.

What football game is for sore oozers?
The Fester Bowl.

Separate Tables
1958

What did the intellectual think about her
spendthrift spouse?
"He'll be the rumination of me!"

What are the first two pages of a malicious tell-all?
The Table of Contempts.

Arms and the Man
1958

What did Susan's homicidal masseur do?
Shiatsu.

Why did Ford invent the assembly line
after watching Netflix?
He said: "The hand-made's stale."

Anatomy of a Murder
1959

Why did the gory adult film "bomb" at the box office?
It wasn't up to snuff.

Why socialize with a jocular hangman?
To learn gallows humor.

Room at the Top
1959

What do you do about heavy breathing in the
upper train compartment?
Call a Pullman-ologist.

Who was the kindliest monarch?
Ben IX.

The Apartment
1960

Why was the homebuilder charged with
sexual harassment?
He made a bungle-low.

What did the Hanoi couple do in their flat
on New Year's?
They had a Tet-a-Tet.

Sons and Lovers
1960

Why did he succeed his father as CEO?
He followed suit.

What didn't he enjoy about his "honey"?
Her hives.

Virgin Spring
1960

Who carefully reads "Orgasms for Dummies"?
Newcomers.

Is it true that oral sex makes you live longer?
No, that's a phallus-y.

Fanny
1961

What did Bette Davis say in the Metamucil commercial?
"What a dump!"

Who is Dr. Chuckle's digestive consultant?
Perry Stall-Sits.

The Hustler
1961

What did the greedy lender have?
A lien and hungry look.

"Why didn't you pay your monthly aikido dues?"
"I have no dough, Joe."

The Important Man
1961

How did Dr. Chuckle show his expertise?
He pundit.

Why did the sheriff plant shrubs in neat rows?
He liked lawn order.

Through A Glass Darkly
1961

What was the global warming expert doing
as the glacier melted?
Scathing on thin ice.

What's the Grim Reaper's favorite frozen dessert?
Pop Sickles.

The Music Man
1962

What did the Vivaldi enthusiast tell
the diehard Wagner fan?
"If it ain't baroque, don't fixate!"

Who is a leading Bach musicologist?
Aaron Agee-Spring.

To Kill a Mockingbird
1962

Why did the songbird mate so often?
He liked to be in at the finch.

Water-bird haiku:
Though I led her-on,
She feels no bittern-nest, so
I have no egrets.

America America
1963

What did Old McDonald say when he called 911?
"ER ER Oh!"

Why did the thug apply for a floor job at Wal-Mart?
He heard they wanted assails person.

How the West Was Won
1963

Who wrote the ancient Chinese book of bronco busting?
Yee Ha!

Who engineered the coup at Tombstone?
Wyatt Usurp.

Lilies of the Field
1963

Why did the botanist collect Hungarian rhapsodies?
They were on her Fronds List.

This old 'ag walks into a piano bar, and the piano player
says: "Witch song you want to hear?
Shall I crone you a melody?"
"Yes, I want Rock of Ags, even though it's a lotta crop."

My Fair Lady
1964

What is a frequent cause of bulimia?
Sylphish motives.

Who is the leading authority on heartburn?
Dr Anne Tacit.

Dr Strangelove
1964

Who diagnoses what's eating you?
Dr Hannah Balekter.

Who performs vaginal tucks in New Delhi?
Dr Kama Suture.

The Sound of Music
1965

How did she listen to the old phono
record of South Pacific?
On Pinza needles.

What composer moonlighted as a sarcastic theatre critic?
Showpan.

Darling
1965

How did she greet guests in her hallway?
Vest-ebulliently.

What was Casanova's theme song?
"I Want a Sundry Kind of Love."

Blood on the Land
1965

What is the most common occupational
hazard for blacksmiths?
Hammer-oids.

How did eating scarecrows cause bleeding?
It's the straw that broke the cannibal's backside.

Dear John
1965

What did the Chinese ship's cook ask the
saucy shore worker?
"A-Hoisin?"

What did she think of his cheap, musky aftershave?
She dismissed it as "spoorious".

Ship of Fools
1965

When was the Know Nothing movement in vogue?
During the ante-cerebellum era.

Where do pirates buy their snazzy socks?
Argh Isle.

A Thousand Clowns
1965

When are frumpy sweatshirts worn?
At Dowdy Hoodie time.

What did the clown ask his daughter?
"Do you have a beau, Zoe?"

The Russians Are Coming!
1966

Which was the most secretive Soviet insect?
The cagey bee.

Who was the most scornful Russian leader?
Czar Kastik.

A Man for All Seasons
1966

What do some herbalists do in December?
They celebrate Arnica.

"People say that you're two-faced."
"That's just a visage rumor!"

A Man and A Woman
1966

What did the maître d' say to his lover?
"Bone Appetit!"

What was the subject of his innuendo?
Her hinterlands.

Fireman's Ball
1966

"Some toxic ex-lover set my bed on fire."
"It might be arson, Nick, from old lays."

What is a massage therapist's favorite hot rock group?
The Iliotibial Band.

Live for Life
1967

What do condom salespersons do for leisure?
Play a rubber of bridge.

"Whath tho thpiritual about Thpecial K?"
"Well, ith ethereal!"

In the Heat of the Night
1967

Where did Dracula dispose of his trampy girlfriends?
On a vamp pyre.

What playwright clumsily ogled women?
Maxim Gawky.

The Graduate
1967

Who is the skipper for the Semester-at-Sea?
Cap'n Gowan.

Who is the most loquacious "suit" on campus?
The gabber-dean.

Guess Who's Coming to Dinner
1967

Why did the mushroom gourmet smirk?
She had a shiitake-eating grin.

Who has an insatiable craving for eating Smurfs?
Bluetooth.

Funny Girl
1968

What did she get from scarfing Czech food?
A Prague in the throat.

In what restoration comedy does an Amazon
do battle with a midget?
"She Stoops to Conk Her."

Stolen Kisses
1968

When do people enjoy rough sex?
When push comes to shove.

What did the hooker send to her favorite clients?
A "Dear John" letter.

Hello, Dolly
1969

What did the soup chef say to the sushi waitress?
"Miso horny!"

What did Ginger do when he stepped on her toes?
She gave Fred a stare.

Five Easy Pieces
1970

Which long-missing musical opus was just found?
Haydn's Seek symphony.

Hear about the tenor whose voice cracked
during the opera?
He was hung in F and G.

The French Connection
1971

"My Paris publisher wants a cheesy novel
about a scary woman."
"Maybe write about the Gorgon, Zola."

Who was the most obese member of the Foreign Legion?
A soldier of portion.

The Last Picture Show
1971

Art critic: "Hue, there's something shady
about your past tints."
Indignant artist (in thought bubble):
"I wonder what that pigment…?"

How do you make treats for Lassie?
With Fi-dough.

The Godfather
1972

How did the godfather show respect?
He tipped his capos.

Mafioso: "Eh, tu capisc'?"
Nerd: "Yes thanks, in the urinal."

Deliverance
1972

For whom did the doctor recommend enemas??
Her constipatients.

Name the best clean-up by the NYC
Department of Sanitation.
The Miracle on Turdy-Turd Street.

Cries and Whispers
1973

How did the audience treat the mediocre comedian?
They raised their heckles; they gave him three jeers.

Why was the contentious lawyer cited for contempt?
She added insult to a jury.

The Sting
1973

"Wie geht's?"
"Es ist nicht tomatensaft!"

Why didn't she accept the free trip to Transylvania?
She was Balkan at the offer.

The Exorcist
1973

How did Geppetto cure Pinocchio?
He used a de-fib-rillator.

How do smart-asses expel evil spirits?
They make wise cracks.

A Touch of Class
1973

Who is Dr. Chuckle's favorite operatic conductor?
Anne Vilkoris.

In olden days, who had toilet seats?
Only the privy-ledged.

Chinatown
1974

Who wears a plumed hat and serves chow mein?
Yangtze Noodle Dandy.

Who wrote the Chinese classic, "Alternatives to Rice"?
Keen Wah.

The Deluge
1974

What does it cost for a creepy-crawly urine sample?
Oh, about a cent a peed.

In which novel is sewage discharged into the ocean?
'20,000 Leaks Under the Sea'.

The Conversation
1974

When did the urologist visit her CPA?
At the end of the piss-call year.

What did the artist's audiologist tell him?
"I observe lots of ear whacks, Vincent."

One Flew Over the Cuckoo's Nest
1975

Why was the starting pitcher ejected from the ballgame?
He relieved himself on the mound.

Why did Imelda give so many footwear parties?
She was fete-ish.

Scent of a Woman
(Italian film)
1975

Why did she wear a highway marker as jewelry?
It was a milestone around her neck.

How did the cashier catch counterfeit coins?
She just was biting her dime.

Dog Day Afternoon
1975

"Do you like the photos of my dog chasing the ball?"
"Oh yes, very fetching."

How did they feel in August when their
fridge suddenly died?
There wasn't a dry ice in the house.

Jaws
1975

"When you gonna finish cookin' them frog legs?"
"A long toad sundown."

She: "I hate to carp, but something was fishy about
your dinner invitation."
He: "Are you being koi with me?"

Rocky
1976

Was she attracted to the rock climber?
No, she found him quite rappelling.

What's kohlrabi?
Heisting 16 tons.

Bound for Glory
1976

Whose immortal plays are best read in a mirror?
The Drab of Nova.

Who is the leading literary Zola scholar?
Jack Hughes.

Taxi Driver
1976

What is the slogan of the leading auto title lender?
"Car Pay Diem!"

Why did the cabbie stop at the produce stand?
To take a leek.

The Goodbye Girl
1977

"Why did you stop dating the mummy?"
"Oh, he's just too wrapped up in himself!"

Who wrote "Guide to Successful Bankruptcy"?
Frieda Detz.

That Obscure Object of Desire
1977

Why was she intimate only with close
friends and neighbors?
She liked to kith and tell.

When did his partner notice that he lacked a foreskin?
At first glans.

The Turning Point
1977

Who exits before toll booths?
Turn-pikers.

What did the coach tell the sprinter who
pulled a side muscle?
"You have oblique prospects."

An Unmarried Woman
1978

What did the cricket player give his lover?
His sticky wicked.

Why did the couple meet only for quickies?
It was an on-and-off relationship.

Midnight Express
1978

Which railroad had the little engine that couldn't?
Lackawanna.

Who is usually the first to leave a party,
well before curfew?
Wanda Roth and Hedda Nowt.

Heaven Can Wait
1978

"The devil is in the details."
"Kindly e-lucifer-date that remark."

Where is Yorick nowadays?
In the scullery.

Breaking Away
1979

Why did the bondsman use a spreadsheet?
To tote that bail.

What do gaucho toddlers do?
They ride on the Pampers.

A Simple Story
1979

"This hog trough is like a silt purse!"
"Yes, it's a real dregs trip."
"My sediments exactly."

Why did she write her autobiography in crayon?
Her life was a no-pen book.

All That Jazz
1979

What did Lawrence Welk refuse to play?
The Strip Polka.

What did the homicidal choir boy do?
He took a stabat mater.

Ordinary People
1980

Why did he become a chimney sweep, like his father?
He wanted to follow soot.

Who is the most bungling mechanic?
Lew Swire.

Confidence
1980

How do mediocre proofreaders enjoy their work?
They have no compliants.

Why did she use "should" so often?
She was ought-istic.

Raging Bull
1980

Who said, "Why don't you two fight?"
A meddle-urge-ist.

When is the best time to roughhouse?
During middle "h".

Chariots of Fire
1981

Why do drivers enter demolition derbies?
For wreck-creation.

Why did the arsonist drive a Welcome Wagon?
To bring "acetylene" gift.

On Golden Pond
1981

How do scholars study 'Walden'?
Thoreau-ly.

What made the retired veterinarian so blunt?
She called a spayed a spayed.

Man of Iron
1981

Who was the dyslexic's favorite Robin Hood strongman?
Fire Truck.

A Great Chinese iron chef said:
"Pork best cooked using KY; Otherwise chop stick!"

Reds
1981

Who said: "Boris, you know what you
can do with that oar!"
The Vulgar Boatman.

What is a messy Soviet's favorite Tchaikovsky piece?
March Slob.

E.T.
1982

What did the horny ET say upon landing?
"Take me to your Lolita."

Where did the dyslexic ET practice PT?
In a teepee.

Private Life
1982

Why should men avoid counterfeit Viagra?
It's not boner-fide.

Where did the birdwatcher spy a woodpecker?
On Pinocchio, of course!

The Verdict
1982

What does Lady Justice hold in her hand?
A statutory rapier.

Who was punished by the gods for playing
with his hot flames?
Promiscuous.

Missing
1982

Whose fillings were lost in Beijing?
Chew In-Lay.

Who is Dr. Chuckle's staff narcoleptic?
Nadeh Doff.

To Begin Again
1982

How are meetings of androids conducted?
They use Robots' Rules of Order.

Where do loutish youngsters enroll in kindergarten?
At rudimentary school.

Terms of Endearment
1983

What toast did the bookie make?
"Here's to bettor days!"

How was phone sex before cell phones?
It was to dial for.

The Big Chill
1983

How did the Headless Horseman travel?
He rode a nightmare.

"That was a great concert, Tina."
"Accordion to whom?"

Entre Nous
1983

How do prison guards communicate?
They talk turnkey.

What plagued early Dutch painters?
Vermeerial disease.

The Dresser
1983

Why did he wear a jockstrap to shop for used cars?
To protect against lowballing.

Why did they use shoddy costumes to
do the medieval epic?
It was Beowulf in cheap clothing.

The Right Stuff
1983

Is Dr. Chuckle familiar with the Law of Averages?
By no means!

Why did Ponce de Leon think that the
Fountain of Youth was in Florida?
He had heard that it was full of Seminole fluid.

Dangerous Moves
1984

What do Japanese chefs in Naples do in their idle time?
They play hibachi-ball.

How did Van Gogh supplement his art income?
With severance pay.

Amadeus
1984

What did Mozart say admiringly to his mistress?
"You have a cozy fan, Tootie."

What is a claque?
The Fandom of the Opera.

Out of Africa
1985

Why didn't the food judges like the pastries
at the County Fair?
They deemed them "ear-elephant".

Where are some babies conceived in West Africa?
In the rear of Dakar.

The Color Purple
1985

If you'd ever seen a purple cow, what did it do?
Mooed indigo.

What Scottish nobleman was repeatedly
stabbed by Macbeth?
The Thane of Groans.

Witness
1985

What was the police officer doing under the bridge?
She was on Pa Troll.

How did she feel when her British lawyer donned a wig?
It em-barrister.

A Room with a View
1986

What did the cathedral architect do on her computer?
She designed the apse.

Why did the young astronomer go to a Parliament debate?
She wanted to observe a Tory.

The Mission
1986

Diogenes was searching for an honest man. Who was searching for a dishonest woman?
His brother, Erogenes.

"Does your charity rely on small donations?"
"That hasn't benefactor."

Moonstruck
1987

What crime did the rock-throwing volcanologist commit?
Felonious basalt.

Why did the astronomer avoid cheese casseroles?
He had a stratas-fear.

Fatal Attraction
1987

Why should you avoid spoiled food?
Taint good fer ya.

Who is the most inexperienced coroner?
Jedediah Knott.

Rain Man
1988

Where do you get your weight, your fortune
and an assessment?
On the autism scale.

Why do they wear rain garb at the
annual urologists' picnic?
It's held under a giant can o' pee.

Working Girl
1988

What did the excavator tell his nagging girlfriend?
"Get off my back, ho!"

How did she greet her favorite florist?
"Hiya, Cynth."

The Accidental Tourist
1988

Who howls at night on roads in the Pyrenees?
The hound of the Basque-curve ills.

How did he like the choppy waters off Scandinavia?
They made him Norse-Sea-ated.

Dangerous Liaisons
1988

What do nihilists say when introduced?
"Pleased to Nietzsche."

Why did the argumentative cannibal
have stomach cramps?
She ate someone that disagreed with her.

Dead Poets Society
1989

What do necrophiliacs enjoy from their partners?
Rolling over in their graves (or inter-corpse.)

What was Oscar Wilde's favorite confection?
A farcical.

Field of Dreams
1989

Why didn't Don Quixote rob banks?
He wilted at mint tills.

"Why aren't you out riding your nice
yellow-and-green tractor?"
"I'm on the john, dear!"

My Left Foot
1989

Who fixed Ted Williams' broken left arm in 1950?
The Splendid Splint-er.

Who made Luke Skywalker's metal hand?
The Lost-End Foundry.

Dances with Wolves
1990

What was the dyslexic's favorite TV show?
Dancing with the Tsars.

What company's logo features
Quasimodo and a werewolf?
Bell and Howl.

Awakenings
1990

Why did he quit his job in the mattress factory?
He wasn't a bedding man.

Who composed the "Clap One Hand March"?
George M. Koan.

Ghost
1990

What did the lepers leave in the pews?
Laity fingers.

What prognosis did the eye surgeon give
the attorney, and why?
"Cyst and decease!" (It was an abscess of malice.)

Open Doors
1990

Why did the chemist become a checker
at a produce store?
She knew Avocado's Number.

Why did the sailor aim his spyglass at the brothel?
He hoped to see the far whore risin'.

The Nasty Girl
1990

Why didn't she patronize the leading tonsil clinic?
Their adenoid her.

Why was the sausage maker lurking
outside the jewelry store?
She was casing the joint.

Goodfellas
1990

How did the police nab the cellphone theft ring?
Sam sung.

How did the banjo player warm up for the concert?
He bluegrass.

Beauty and the Beast
1991

What is bestiality?
It's leading a lamb to the slutter.

What's the dermatological term for scaly shins?
"A site for psoriasis."

Bugsy
1991

Why don't termite-eaters have time to play?
It can be aardvark.

What did Norman Bates admit at the end of 'Psycho'?
"Mother is the invention of necessity!"

The Prince of Tides
1991

What do octopi proudly display?
Their coats of arms.

Why was the beach strewn with pairs of Adidas?
From a sneaker wave.

Unforgiven
1992

Why did the serial killer wed the arsonist?
It was a deranged marriage.

Who makes a career writing regret notes?
Morse Dapitti.

A Few Good Men
1992

What was the cannibal's favorite table game?
Ate-ball (though it gave him a slightly billiards feeling).

Why did Marx have such a big following?
He knew all the Engels.

Scent of a Woman
1992

What did Mary Shelley tell her poet husband, Percy?
"I like your body, oder."

What did Quasimodo do before his big date?
He gargoyled Listerine.

The Crying Game
1992

Where in the Bible can you read sad words
about plywood?
The Laminations of Jeremiah.

Which ape goes on tirades?
The harangue-utan.

The Fugitive
1993

How did the master criminal receive
an honorary doctorate?
The police gave him the third degree.

What did she yell when her dentures were being stolen?
"Stop, teeth!"

In the Name of the Father
1993

What did they call the talented, rising young cleric?
"Your Imminence."

What are parsnips?
What Dad drank surreptitiously.

The Piano
1993

How did Liberace die?
He was done in by his piano tumor.

Who wrote songs about kangaroos?
Walt Sigma Tilden.

The Remains of the Day
1993

How long does it take to reach your
lawyer while she's golfing?
An attorney-tee.

Who looks gift horses in the mouth?
*Requestrians. (Or, perhaps,
eye-denticle twins or geld-diggers?)*

Quiz Show
1994

Where are Colonel Sanders' chicken crumbs?
In his goat-tea.

"Didn't that great Swedish skier win
the Olympic slalom in 1956?"
"No, something's rotten in your date of Stenmark!"

Eat Drink Man Woman
1994

Why didn't Toulouse imbibe at the Moulin Rouge?
The bar was set too high.

What exploded in the Indian restaurant?
The blow-up daal.

Dust of Life
1995

What waif toils in a dirty coal mine?
Ore-fan Black.

Why didn't the tourist wear a sun helmet in the tropics?
He was pith poor.

Braveheart
1995

Why does Superman nab runaway chickens
and mad scientists?
*He is faster than a speeding pullet and stronger
than a loco motive.*

Who has artificial body parts and writes epic poems?
The Byronic Man.

Sense and Sensibility
1995

Who are the two most prominent female diplomats?
Polly Titian and Emma Seri.

What do smart cars use to avoid fender benders?
A collide-a-scope.

Ridicule
1996

"Ever hear about Quasimodo?"
"What a stoop-ed question!"

What is the leading book about animal husbandry?
'Beauty and the Beast'.

Secrets & Lies
1996

In which Shakespeare play do "false facts" win out?
'The Shaming of the True'.

What is a frequent scam at the Vatican?
The PayPal bull.

Titanic
1997

What did she tell her seasick spouse?
"Does that drama mean that you forgot your meds?"

Who designed the Titanic?
The foundering fathers.

As Good as It Gets
1997

What did the sleepy Spoonerist love to do?
Take warty finks.

Of what do Japanese gluttons dream?
Perpetual mochi.

The Full Monty
1997

What did the stripper do after overeating for the holidays?
She tried to take it all off.

What do exhibitionists display?
Their points of view.

Character
1997

Who is the only person not on Facebook?
Liv–Mia Loan.

What do repo men do during school hours?
They play hooky.

Life Is Beautiful
1998

What happens after the afterglow?
The anticlimax.

Who was the most agreeable monarch?
William the Concurrer.

American Beauty
1999

What did the baker tell his sweetie?
"I've got a crust on you."

Why did the dominatrix carry a blue-green whip?
She had a mind like a teal strap.

The Insider
1999

Why didn't he have an opinion on female circumcision?
He had no foreskin in the game.

Why did he never go camping?
He had a tent shun disorder.

Gladiator
2000

Who was the greatest nomadic heroine?
Wander Woman.

Who is the oldest active hockey star?
Gerry Hattrick.

Traffic
2000

What did the inexperienced groper say?
"I'm a stranger in these parts."

Why are people jailed for selling fake Saran?
It's a bum wrap.

The Taste of Others
2000

What did the thug ask his dinner partner?
"Care to eat more roughy, Anne?"

How did he prepare such nauseating meals?
He used a queasy-n-art.

Everybody's Famous!
2000

What organization uses the Elephant Man
as its poster child?
The Anti-Deformation League.

Who was the most leisurely repenter?
Marian Haste.

A Beautiful Mind
2001

Who was King Arthur's wise man?
Sir Rebral.

What caused the uproar in the computer lab?
A pinched nerd.

In the Bedroom
2001

Who sat on Mr Potato Head?
Min Stunyan.

What did the agronomist do with his lab assistant?
He soiled him.

The Pianist
2002

Why was the composer imprisoned?
For his fugue-in de minor.

What pieces did Debussy write consecutively?
Éclair de la Lune, followed by La Merde.

The Hours
2002

"We need to meet soon to combat brain-drain."
"Okay, I'll mark it on my colander."

What did the ravenously hungry timekeeper do?
Eight o'clock (then asked for seconds).

The Barbarian Invasions
2003

What did the gangster's loyal enforcer do?
Maimed to please.

What rodent burrows into sewer pipes?
The toilet vole.

Lost in Translation
2003

What did Tonto say at the Tijuana cancer clinic?
"Me here for cheap chemo, sabe?"

How do folks from Rapid City understand Alabamans?
The use a South Decoder.

Master and Commander
2003

What happens when you tell lies to the thunder god?
True Thor consequences.

What did the ref say to the trash-talking basketball players?
"Silence on the Court!"

Yesterday
2004

What's the most boring part of the Constitution?
"Ennui the people..."

What do Scriptures say about black-and-blue marks?
"Their name is Lesion."

The Aviator
2004

Why did the aviatrix abort takeoff?
Her rise was bigger than her tarmac.

How did the airline baker fare when she took up juggling?
She came through with flying crullers.

Sideways
2004

How did the dyslexic settle his bar tab?
He gave the bartender his "itch".

How do you anger a railroad tycoon?
Interrupt his thought of train.

The Sea Inside
2004

Why didn't he hear about the French fish sauce?
Meunière's disease.

Who eats raw fish and collects monsters?
The Poke Mon.

Finding Neverland
2004

What do the Living Dead drive?
Corpse-sicles.

What was the bird watcher expecting in the End Times?
The Raptor.

Good Night and Good Luck
2005

Why did the hermit crab so much?
He spent all day on his big grump; he cave at the orifice.

Why didn't the gambler use a condom?
He liked to play rush-in roulette.

Crash
2005

When did the multiple-staircase structure implode?
During the Fall of the House of Escher.

Body-shop worker: "That's the way the
cookie truck crumples."
Co-worker: "That's the way the Mercedes bends."

The Departed
2006

How did the descending mountaineers fall into the abyss?
The hole was crater than the summit departs.

What did the cemetery vandals do?
They left no stone unturned.

The Queen
2006

"What became of your cousin, Bee?"
"Very tragic, the pollinator!"

Was Queen Victoria able to stay relaxed to the very end?
No, she passed tense.

Water
2006

What do ship stokers wear around town?
Their sooty slickers.

Why didn't the whale ever leap?
He was too big for his breaches.

The Lives of Others
2006

Who does martial arts and is a royal pain in the neck?
The Carotid Kid.

Who constructs houses with appliances included?
Bill Tin.

Babel
2006

"Wadi singing about?"
"Oman river, that Oman river...."

How do you interrupt a nonstop talker?
Forget it! You don't have a chime-in man's chance.

There Will Be Blood
2007

What is a turnip?
The result of petting a certain seabird.

What was Dracula's sexual preference?
He was a hemo- sexual.

Departures
2008

What's the start of a famous dyslexic saying?
"If the hose fist...."

"Are you telling me that spiny anteaters really lay eggs?"
"Echidna not."

The Reader
2008

What is fittingly named for use as outhouse paper?
Reader's Digest.

Why did King John cite the Old Testament
before signing the Magna Carta?
He said: "Deuteronomy before Runnymede do to you!"

The Blind Side
2009

Oedipus went insane and blinded himself.
What's the moral?
"Out of sight, out of mind."

"I think nearsighted Mr. Magoo is hysterical!"
"How dare you marginal-eyes him!
(Remarks like that just Backus up!)"

An Education
2009

"Why don't they teach us about curries
in this culinary school?"
"Be patient. You're only a first-termer, Rick."

"Do you realize that 'testament' comes from
the same root as 'testicle'?"
"I think you've slipped a cog, Nate."

A Serious Man
2009

How did he respond when she crumpled up his ugly hat?
"Wadded you do that for?"

What did the irate spouse tell Brahms' buddy?
"Keep Johannes offa my woman!"

Up
2009

"I built castles in the air."
"You rectum, too!"

Why did the cannibal leap into the pot?
To make something of himself.

Up in the Air
2009

What did the hygienist give to the non-flossing patient?
Dental flak.

Who was Ferdinand?
A famous bull-dozer.

Inglourious Basterds
2009

Who was the Nazi's favorite pin-up girl?
Barb Aryan.

What precipitated the Trojan Wars?
Condom nations.

The Kids Are All Right
2010

Where do you find pictures of pot-smoking athletes?
On boxes of Weedies.

Which Dean Martin lines did the
cannibal hum while cooking?
"Three little kids for the flavor…"

The King's Speech
2010

What gift did the King of Norway offer to Ophelia?
Four tin bras.

Why does the Navy hire speech therapists?
Because "loose lisps think ships!"

The Social Network
2010

"Take me to the soiree; I'm getting stale
from sitting around."
"But the party's stag, Nancy."

What's a rhubarb?
An online insult aimed at a yokel (e.g. "How's your jicama?")

In a Better World
2010

Why are some people so relaxed?
They have a tension-deficit.

Who works at nauseating jobs?
People in the gag economy.

True Grit
2010

How did she curse so friskily?
She was feeling her oaths.

Why did the thief indiscreetly boast about his jobs?
He has a "trap" like a steal mind.

Inception
2010

Who invented pate de foie gras?
A French organ-grinder.

Who dreamed up Prohibition?
Bruno Hooch.

Outside the Law
2010

What did the police do after the break-in at McDonald's?
They grilled a burglar.

How did the dog breeder become a voyeur?
He had a peekin' ease.

Footnote
2011

Where do obit writers like to meet for lunch?
On Pasta Way.

What is the EPA's ideal?
Emission impossible.

The Artist
2011

What became of the octogenarian nude model?
She retired to the drawing room.

Why did Tchaikovsky put honey and pecans on his saltines?
He liked his nut crackers sweet.

The Descendants
2011

What proportion of afterbirths are
consumed by the mother?
Only a small placenta of them.

What did the midwife do to her arch-rival?
She challenged her to a doula.

The Help
2011

Why did the customer ask the young cashier
for a birth certificate?
He wanted to be sure that she was "legal" and tender.

Who is Dr. Chuckle's favorite waiter?
Javier D. Seided.

The Tree of Life
2011

How do you do triage?
You count the rings on the trunk.

Why did the couple build a treehouse?
They wanted to live off the land.

Midnight in Paris
2011

Where was the deserter on D-Day?
Hiding in a bidet.

What is the ecological danger from gorging on crudités?
The dreaded greenhouse-gas effect!

Les Misérables
2012

Who was guillotined for pimping?
The headless whore's-man.

Who is Dr Chuckle's staff masochist?
Winston Payne.

American Hustle
2013

What do chronic complainers do?
They make new whines from old gripes.
(They put new whines into old battles.)

How can you best use three minutes?
Read a soft-boiled detective story.

Her
2013

What do you call someone who makes love when confused?
Adelaide.

"I hear that you broke a leg bone."
"That's just a fib, Beulah!"

Gravity
2013

What did they give the runner-up in
the astronomy competition?
The constellation prize.

What is a pumpkin?
A relative of a syphon.

Birdman
2014

Which Renaissance painting depicts
birds' bizarre activities?
Aberration of the Magpie.

Who is the fish hawk's favorite entertainer?
"The Grand Ol' Osprey."

The Theory of Everything
2014

What's the status of her two novellas
about the Second Coming?
They're forthcoming.

How did Miss Muffet cure her arachnophobia?
She vowed to tuffet out.

American Sniper
2014

What did the critic say about the half-empty theatre?
"Pardon me, but your show is slipping."

Patient: "It's a dull pain somewhere in my mouth."
Dentist: "Are you being ob-tooth?"

Whiplash
2014

Who totaled his car while going down on his girlfriend?
Oedipussy Wrecks.

What was her defense against a charge of drunk driving?
She pleaded the fifth.

Boyhood
2014

Who apprenticed for the Prince of Darkness?
Idle Hans.

How do droids remain youthful-looking?
They use Robotox.

The Imitation Game
2014

What game does a certain peevish politician play?
"Where's wall-dough?"

What are the two favorite sports in the
Dyslexic Winter Olympics?
The "glue" and "chokey".

Wild Tales
2014

Why did the exotic dancer emerge from the giant pastry?
She had fearlessly stepped into the brioche.

Who defeated the Roman army by eating lots of cabbage?
The Toot-ons.

Room
2015

Variation on a childhood riddle: When is a jar not ajar?
When it's adored.

Who has a bureau where he files briefs?
Chester Drawers.

Spotlight
2015

Why did the corpulent teen actress call for help?
She was going through a stage.

Who is the leading maven on coffee etiquette?
Duncan Do-Not.

Arrival
2016

What is a favorite politically incorrect gastro joke?
"So, these two polyps walk into a bar...."

Whose arrival soiled the picnic celebration?
The party pooper. (Did the ants-er surprise you?)

Fences
2016

Farmer 1: "Is your land encumbered?"
Farmer 2: "No, it's cucumbered."

Which store best stymies shoplifters?
F.A.O. Thwarts.

Hell or High Water
2016

What did one Viking say to the other?
"It takes a whole pillage to raze a shire!"

How does the realtor sell beach property
on the Indian Ocean?
"She sells Seychelles: 'Buy the Seashore.'"

Hidden Figures
2016

What are Mumbai counterfeiters up to lately?
Just makin' rupee.

Did Superman attend the nudist poultry dinner?
Yes, but he was chicken, so he had a capon.

The Shape of Water
2017

How did the gardener meet her doom at the Coast?
She was trying to cultivate wild orcas.

Why didn't he tell her that she had body odor?
He was wishy-washy.

Get Out
2017

When was Anne Hutchison expelled from
the Massachusetts Colony?
During a ban-her year.

Why did mastodons become extinct?
Too much masto-baiting.

Darkest Hour
2017

Why did she feel throat tightness about
her former spouse?
It was her ex-tension cord.

Why are there so many depressed sewage workers?
They're down in the dumps.

Phantom Thread
2017

Why do ghosts regularly make appearances?
It's deja boo!

Where do you find the 39 Steps and
angels that fear to tread?
In a stairing contest.

Loveless
2017

How did the origami shop do?
It folded.

How were things for the destitute yoga teacher?
She didn't even have dwi pada pitham.

The Insult
2017

Why don't Puritans read the Kamasutra?
They regard it as a louche canon.

What did the audience do at the premiere
of the bad adult film?
They began steaming for the exits.

A Fantastic Woman
2017

Why did the hospice nurse hire an insulation expert?
She wanted her flatlined.

What did Julius Caesar sing in bed?
"Calpurnia, here I come!"

The Square
2017

What did Euclid exclaim about Sicilian pizza?
"This pie are squared!"

What happened to the belfry of Notre Dame?
It ex-spired.

Lady Bird
2017

What small brown bird often falls off its perch?
The wobbler.

Why did the bird become so stressed?
She said, "Do you know how tough it is to raise a tanager?"

Green Book
2018

What did the knaves do in the produce market?
Wrap scallions.

"Why do so many Brits have green
boogers on their fingers?"
"Nose-picker da English."

A Star Is Born
2018

Which tenor has no impact on the audience?
Placebo Domingo.

Why did the wonk join the opera chorus?
She was hoping to date a bass.

Vice
2018

What do they do on Christmas Eve in dystopian societies?
Sing "Soylent Night."

Where do topless maidens roll in guano?
Lake Titicaca.

The Favourite
2018

Who provides refreshments in central Illinois?
Decatur-er.

What do seafood restaurants serve on hot summer days?
Fishy-ssoise.

Shoplifters
2018

Who scams people on the Farmers Only dating site?
The charmer in the Dell.

Who fanatically steals pun books?
Synonymphomaniacs.

Never Look Away
2018

Why did the cat puke on the rug?
It was a Purgein' carpet.

How was the tear-jerker porn flick rated?
Clean-X.

Cold War
2018

What disabled the cyber-terrorist?
A hacking cough.

Why did the Brexit fanatic visit the doctor?
For a Euroanalysis.

Parasite
2019

How did the debauched grad students
spend their spare time?
Defending their dissipations.

Which Shakespeare play concerns a bothersome
slacker in the gig economy?
The Temp Pest.

Joker
2019

What did Jean Valjean say as he stole a loaf of bread?
"It takes a thief focaccia thief!"

In which Mark Twain novel is a client
white-washed in court?
"The Adventures of Tom's Lawyer".

Marriage Story
2019

What did the incompatible iguanas do?
Anole their marriage.

How do cannibals end marriages?
They consume-mate.

Honeyland
2019

Why is an Ohio team called "the Zips"?
It's an Akron-ism.

What did it cost for a threesome in Czarist Russia?
A couple of copeckers.

Pain and Glory
2019

What's the dominant chain of hemorrhoid clinics?
The Ass-Tech Empire.

What was the sadist's trademark?
His manacle laughter.